Legends and Heroes

Created By

STONE MARSHALL®

With the

STONE MARSHALL® STUDIO

StoneMarshall.com edition Dec 6, 2015
Published by Stone Marshall Publishing

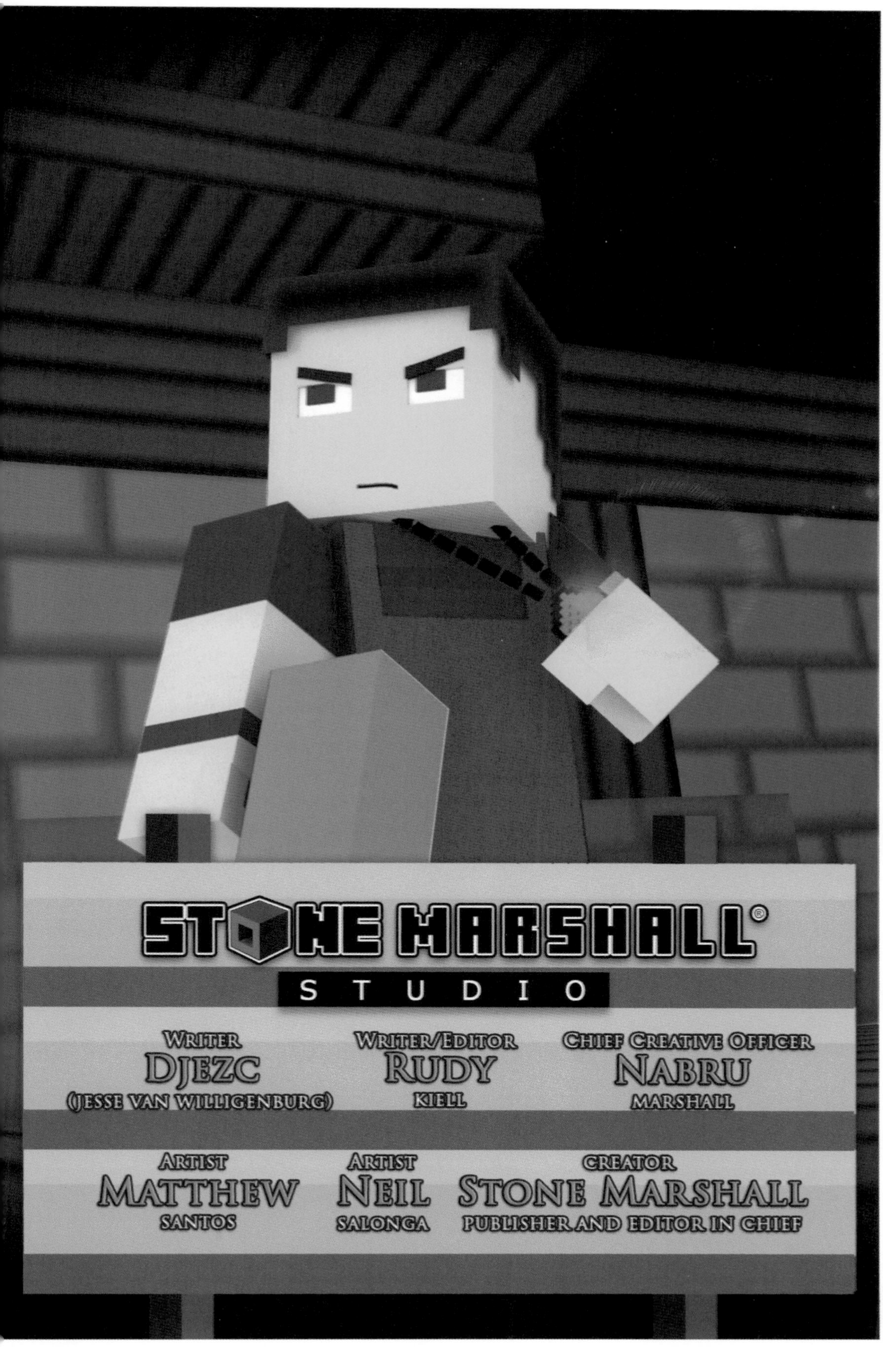
STONE MARSHALL®
STUDIO
WRITER
DJEZC
(JESSE VAN WILLIGENBURG)
WRITER/EDITOR
RUDY
KIELL
CHIEF CREATIVE OFFICER
NABRU
MARSHALL
ARTIST
MATTHEW
SANTOS
ARTIST
NEIL
SALONGA
CREATOR
STONE MARSHALL
PUBLISHER AND EDITOR IN CHIEF

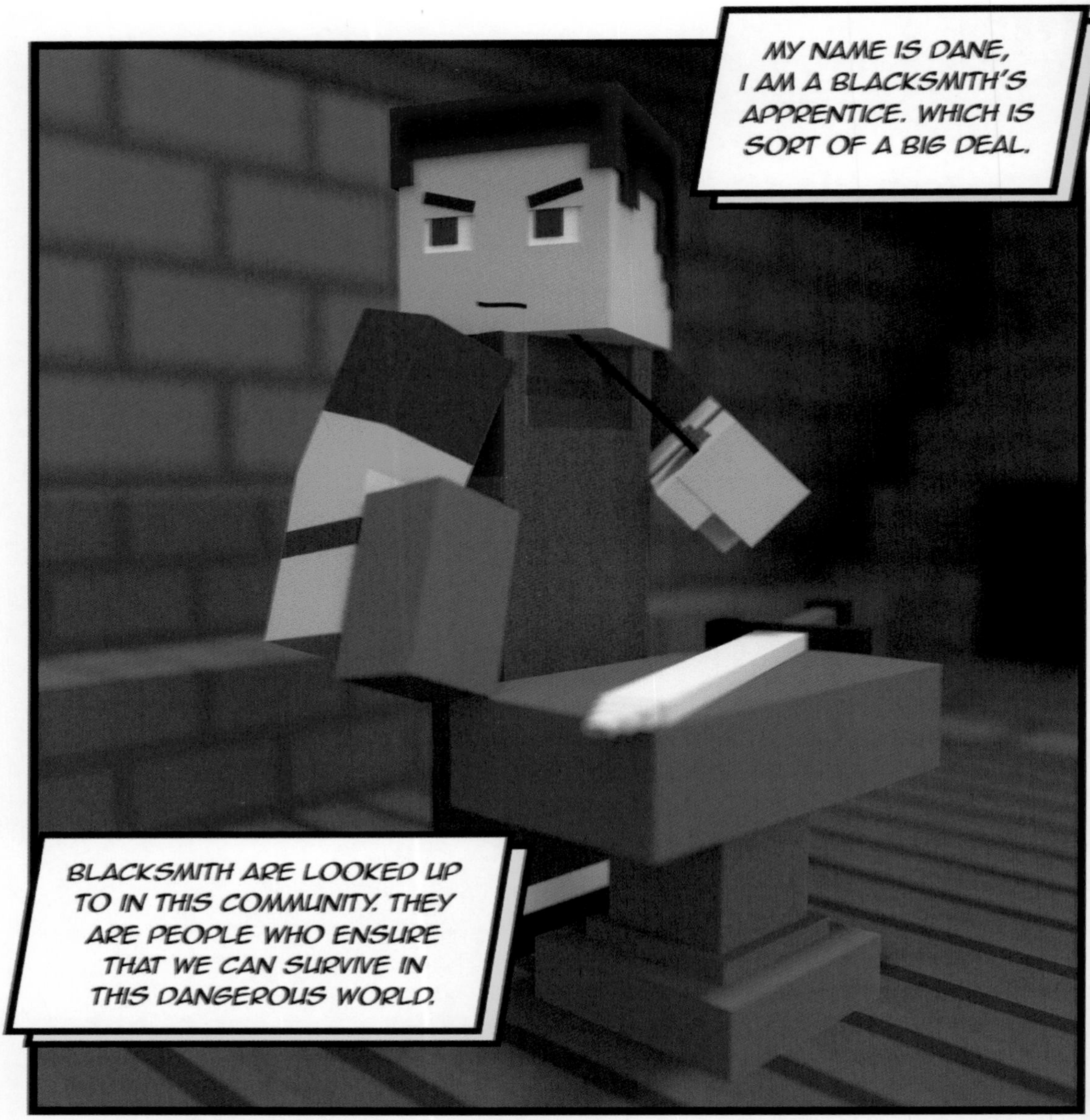
MY NAME IS DANE, I AM A BLACKSMITH'S APPRENTICE. WHICH IS SORT OF A BIG DEAL.
BLACKSMITH ARE LOOKED UP TO IN THIS COMMUNITY. THEY ARE PEOPLE WHO ENSURE THAT WE CAN SURVIVE IN THIS DANGEROUS WORLD.

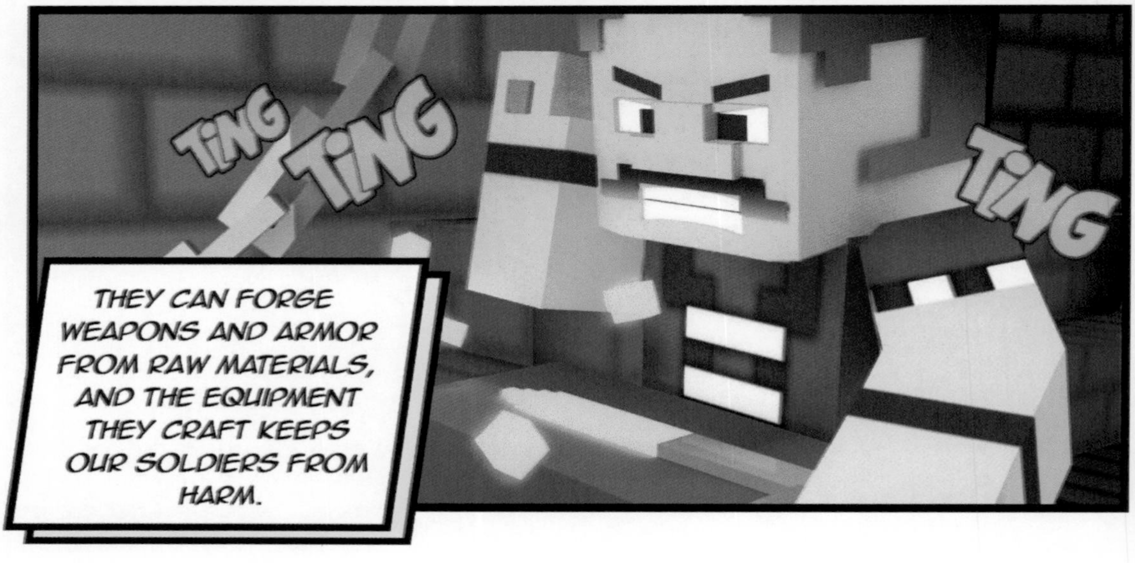
TING
TING
TING
THEY CAN FORGE WEAPONS AND ARMOR FROM RAW MATERIALS, AND THE EQUIPMENT THEY CRAFT KEEPS OUR SOLDIERS FROM HARM.

MY NAME IS DANE. I am a blacksmith's apprentice, which is sort of a big deal. Blacksmiths are looked up to in this community. They are people who ensure that we can survive in this dangerous world. They can forge weapons and armor from raw materials, and the equipment they craft keeps our soldiers from harm.

During the day, this world is beautiful. Huge mountain ranges line every horizon. Endless fields and hills surround dense forests and vast savannahs. Freezing tundra, scorching deserts, and deep blue oceans sweep across the cube, all of them filled with remnants of an ancient civilization.

However, when the sun sets, this world shows another face. Hostile monsters crawl from the shadows and the caves, hunting anyone foolish enough to venture out at night. Giant spiders, reanimated corpses, and cursed skeletons make up only a few of these terrifying creatures. Heroic tales tell of many more, each more sinister than the next.

Recently, the king decreed that every town, village, and city should have a city guard: a garrison of trained warriors to ensure that we can sleep peacefully at night. Supplying the city guard with weapons and armor are blacksmiths, who have trained their entire lives to be able to turn raw stone, iron, and even diamond into wearable protective equipment.

The town I live in is called Stathmore. Our village might not be large, but it's home to one of the world's best blacksmiths, Viegar. I've heard all kinds of stories about him, all of them filled with adventure and heroism, but Viegar himself is often hesitant to talk about his past.

I know that Viegar was part of the king's inner circle at one point in time, advising the father of our current king on military matters. He now spends his days working the forge and teaching a few lucky people the secrets of his trade. In our small village, away from the big cities he knew for so long, he now lives a tranquil life.

It's perfect for him, but nothing ever happens here. And that is exactly why I would leave this place if I could.

The life of a blacksmith's apprentice is not an easy one, but that doesn't mean it's very exciting either. Every day is the exact same mundane routine: hammer on anvil, stoke the fire, greet customers, make deliveries, and repeat. Guards and adventurers are always in need of new gear, and the blacksmith is happy to provide them. We do repairs on weapons and armor too, but I only get to work with wood, stone, and iron. Viegar takes care of any orders involving diamond. He says I'm not ready for it yet. I've been training as his apprentice, but I always get nothing but boring chores!

"Go repair this sword, Dane."

"Go fetch more wood from the storage, Dane."

"Go make yourself useful, Dane, while I talk with this man over here."

He gets visitors from time to time. Some are well-dressed gentlemen of high standing. Others are soldiers clad in heavy armor, weathered from adventure. I like to imagine just how they got so weathered—what stories lie behind each scar and scrape? By the time I come out of these fantasies, the guests are already gone.

Make no mistake, I really appreciate the opportunity. It is an honor to learn from Viegar. The way he works the forge is miraculous. There is a certain art to his work. He wields the hammer with power, yet elegance. He uses tremendous force, but he does not break things, instead shaping and molding them into all sorts of amazing items.

My father served with him in the royal guard, and they were still good friends until the day my father disappeared, but that's another story. Of course, that is probably the only reason Viegar agreed to take in a dreamer like me as his apprentice!

"Hey, you!" Viegar shouts.

I jump up, suddenly wide awake, and frantically look around at my surroundings. My eyes land on a stout, muscular man standing before the forge. Viegar's dark hair clings to his damp forehead. His mustache is the same color as the ash that seems to cover the smithee's every surface, and it twitches when he's annoyed. As he is now.

"I don't pay you to be dozing off, do I now?" Viegar snaps. "Get back to working the forge! We have work to do, and many orders to fill!"

"Yes sir," I say, shaking off my peaceful nap. "I'll get to it right away!" I walk back to the forge and pump the bellows to stoke the fire.

You can tell immediately that Viegar is a master blacksmith. The man built his own forge, because he thinks normal forges are "inefficient" and "too small-scaled." It's not simply two blocks of lava, but a three-by-five pool of it, surrounded by obsidian rather than stone slabs. Standing on obsidian pillars, a supply of charcoal fuels the fires below, to keep the lava in liquid form. "Normal coal burns unevenly," he once said to me, "charcoal has felt the heat of the flames before."

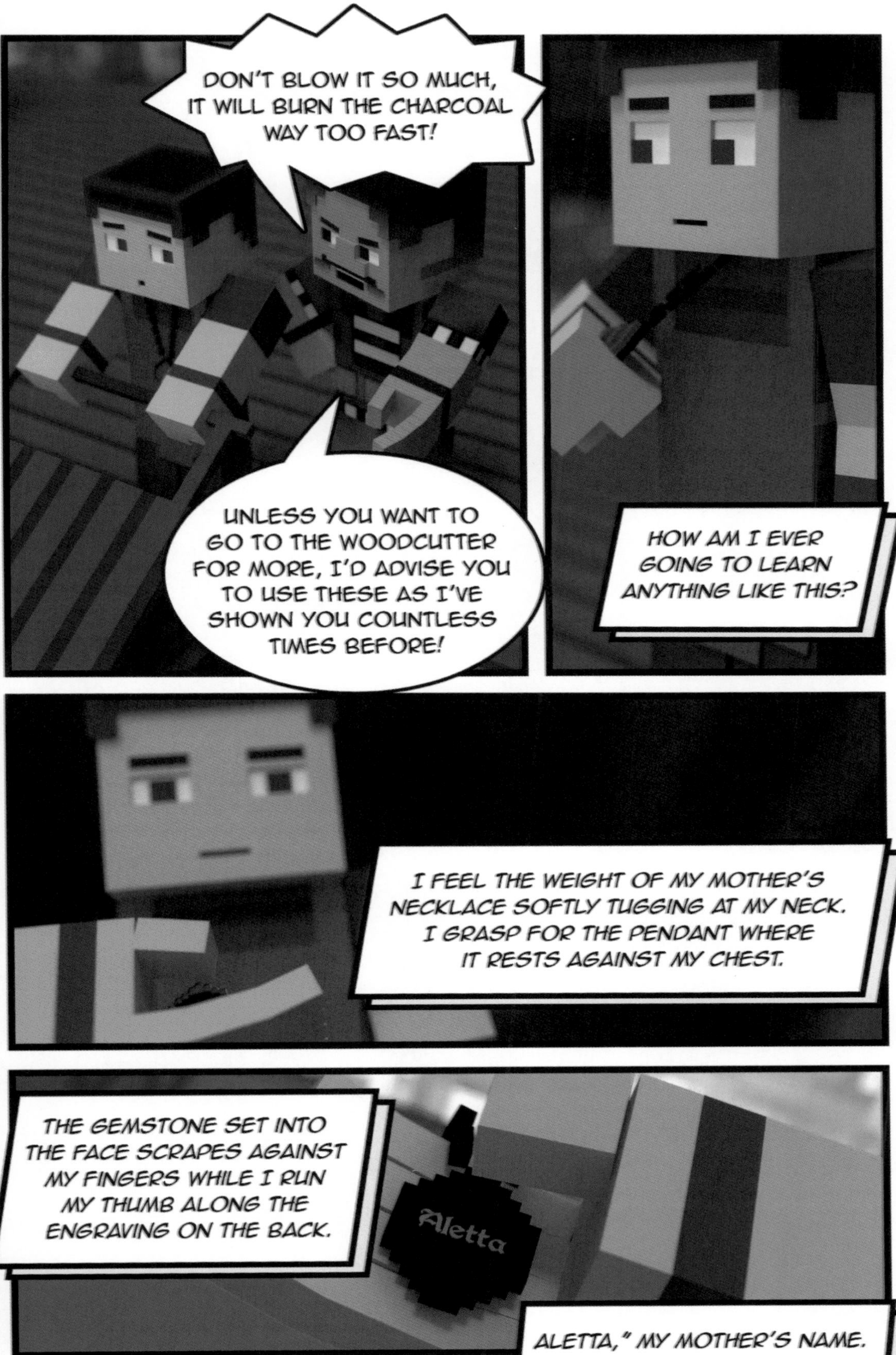
DON'T BLOW IT SO MUCH, IT WILL BURN THE CHARCOAL WAY TOO FAST!
UNLESS YOU WANT TO GO TO THE WOODCUTTER FOR MORE, I'D ADVISE YOU TO USE THESE AS I'VE SHOWN YOU COUNTLESS TIMES BEFORE!
HOW AM I EVER GOING TO LEARN ANYTHING LIKE THIS?
I FEEL THE WEIGHT OF MY MOTHER'S NECKLACE SOFTLY TUGGING AT MY NECK. I GRASP FOR THE PENDANT WHERE IT RESTS AGAINST MY CHEST.
THE GEMSTONE SET INTO THE FACE SCRAPES AGAINST MY FINGERS WHILE I RUN MY THUMB ALONG THE ENGRAVING ON THE BACK.
Aletta
ALETTA," MY MOTHER'S NAME.

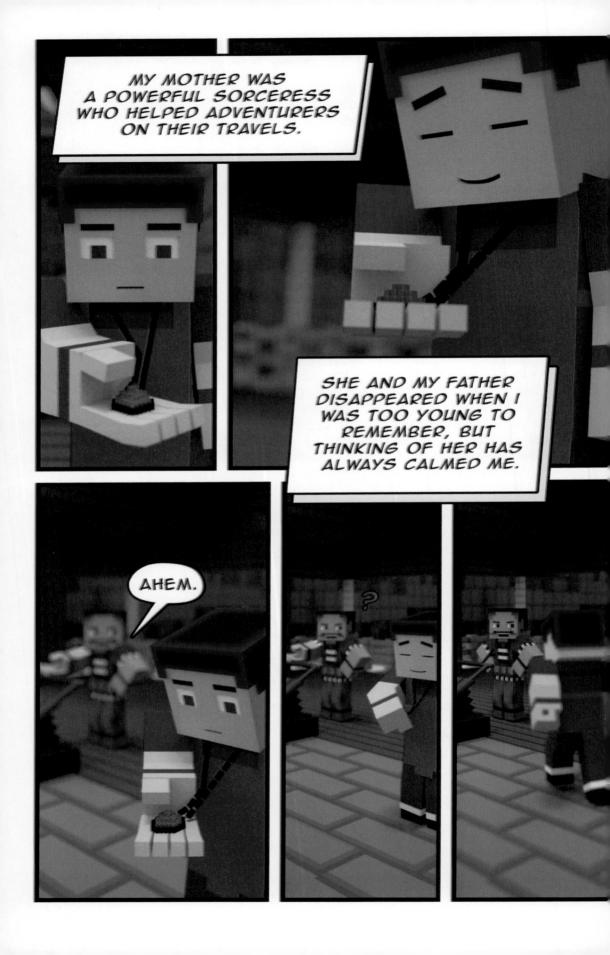

VIEGAR LOOKS UP AND swiftly walks over to me.

"Don't blow it so much, it will burn the charcoal way too fast! Unless you want to go to the woodcutter for more, I'd advise you to use these as I've shown you countless times before!" He pushes me aside and takes over the bellows. As much as I try, I just don't see what he is doing differently.

How am I ever going to learn anything like this? I feel the weight of my mother's necklace softly tugging at my neck. I grasp for the pendant where it rests against my chest. The gemstone set into the face scrapes against my fingers while I run my thumb along the engraving on the back: "Aletta," my mother's name.

My mother was a powerful sorceress who helped adventurers on their travels. She and my father disappeared when I was too young to remember, but thinking of her has always calmed me.

Viegar steps away from the bellows and gestures for me to take over. I give my mother's locket one last squeeze and ask her for patience before I start in again.

As I said before, honorable as it might be, the life of a blacksmith is just not the life for me. Though Viegar is the best blacksmith in the land, I have done nothing to deserve his teachings and, to be honest, I don't really want to learn this trade. I would rather be out there in the world, fighting the creatures that creep from the shadows at night and defending the village from the aimless mutants that lurk past the reach of the torchlight.

But there is a bright side, I suppose. I'm not alone. There is another apprentice, a freckled, redheaded farmer's boy named Snip. Snip is much more talented at smithing than I could ever be, probably because he has the motivation for it. I think he knows that I do not share his love of the job. Nonetheless, he is nice and likes to see everyone treated fairly. He is my friend.

Snip puts down the iron blade he has been quietly sharpening and looks out the window. "Sir, I think the caravan is passing through town again. Would you like me to take the weapons and armor to the soldiers?"

Viegar frowns thoughtfully. "Yes, go ahead, Snip. Try fetching a good price for those chestplates we crafted last week. Tell them we used our best ores to make them. And don't forget to stock up on extra sticks and charcoal."

I watch Snip lift a heavy crate of goods. Just as the front door swings shut behind him, it's pushed open again.

A large man walks in, his shoulder-length, blonde hair hidden under a diamond helmet. He wears a chestplate made of solid diamond, with the royal coat-of-arms on it. On his shoulders rests a cloak that looks like it was spun with golden thread, bearing the same emblem as his chestplate. A diamond sword hangs in a sheath from his belt, both made of high-grade treated leather. I stare at him in amazement. Only one order of knights wear armor of this quality: the Royal Guard.

Only the most valiant of knights and trusted warriors get to join the Royal Guard. The Royal Guard protects the king from his enemies. Although our king is a righteous ruler, like any person of great power, he has enemies. The Royal Guard protects the king and his family from those who would overthrow him and seize his power. But the Royal Guard do more than stay at the king's side, they travel across the land on all manner of quests —from slaying powerful beasts to maintaining order in settlements.

What a life that must be!

Viegar walks up to the Royal Guard and shakes his hand.

"Viegar, my old friend," the knight says, "I see you have not lost your edge when it comes to the smithing trade!"

"Did you expect me to, then, Gavin?" Viegar replies. "I have been a blacksmith for years now; it is what I do best." He sets his weight back and puts his hands on his hips. "Now, to what do I owe the pleasure of the Royal Guard visiting my shop?"

The man smiles, but it doesn't reach his eyes. He seems worried. "A word, please, if you have the time. . ." He glances toward me. "In private."

Viegar hesitates, but does not ask the knight any questions, "I see . . . follow me, then."

I watch them walk away down the hallway, past the item frames where we store our equipment. They enter the cellar and Viegar locks the door behind them. I try to get back to tending the forge, but it isn't long before my curiosity gets the better of me. Snip will be away for quite some time; no one will even notice that I'm gone. I carefully move away from the forge and glance toward the front door to make sure it's still closed. I tiptoe across the squeaky floorboards toward the door.

I try to sneak a peek through the keyhole. Alas, Viegar has left the key in from the other side, so there is not much to see. I softly press my ear against the door, hoping the floorboards will not give my eavesdropping away.

I hear the knight's unfamiliar voice first, "Viegar, I will be honest with you. Since you left, things have gotten bad. I am not one to question the king's judgment, but his new military advisor has trouble keeping things under control. We lost another patrol last night, and last week an entire garrison was overrun. We got most people out of the town in time, but we had to leave some of the sick, old, and wounded. One of our divisions reclaimed it the next day, but it proves a point."

I lose myself in thought again. What an exciting job it must be to travel the lands on a king's orders, helping those in need and fighting evil . . .

"Shadows are stirring, something big is about to happen, and in all honesty, I don't know if we are ready for what's coming, Viegar. Are you sure you're not willing to reconsider rejoining the Royal Guard?"

BANG!

I jump back in surprise at the loud noise on the other side of the door. I quickly press my ear against the door again.

"We have been over this before!" Viegar says loudly. When he speaks again, he speaks softly. I have to strain to hear. "I have made my decision, and there's nothing you can say or do to change my mind. Those days are behind me!"

The knight sighs. "I see you are still as stubborn as the day you left us. If there is no way for me to make you reconsider, so be it. However, I have a favor to ask of you. There is something I need. Something no other blacksmith has been able to do."

There is a small pause. "That is the most interesting metal I've ever seen . . ." Viegar says, his voice even lower than before.

"I need you to forge a weapon from this. Can you do it?"

"It will cost me the rest of the evening," Viegar says thoughtfully, "but I will work all night to have it for you when you leave in the morning."

"I will spend the night here then, if you don't mind. Naturally, I will compensate you. Is that acceptable?"

"It will have to do. You can take my bed; I won't be getting much sleep anyway."

I sense the conversation has ended and quickly, but silently, make my way back to the forge and resume tending it as if I'd never left. The door unlocks and the two walk down the hallway. As I pump the bellows, the knight walks toward me, a smile growing on his face. I'm sure my face is bright red as he offers me a slight bow and removes his helmet. He didn't hear me eavesdropping, did he?

"My name is Gavin, young man," he says cheerfully. "And who might you be, then?"

I struggle to find the words. "Dane, sir. My name is Dane," I finally say. I'm relieved he didn't catch me spying, but I still find it hard to speak to such a magnificent knight.

"That would be one of my two apprentices," Viegar says dismissively. "Speaking of which, I wonder what is taking the other one so long." He steps toward me and waves me away from the bellows. "Dane, I'll take over for now. Go find Snip. I will be working through the night, so I will have need of you again. For now, bring Snip back here, and then see if there are any new traders in the caravan."

"Yes, sir," I say sulkily. Just my luck. I've been stuck inside all day and the moment I get to go outside I'd rather stay with the knight. He must have so many stories to tell . . .

I live in a village of decent size. In the center of our town sits a well that was built on a natural underground spring. The well provides us with clean water that is safe to drink. There are a few farms to provide us with food. It's mostly wheat, carrots, and potatoes, but at least there is plenty. We have a small library, where scholars come to study and people come to read. Just outside the town, the land falls into a quarry where miners dig to collect raw materials, which are always in high demand. There is also a church with a priest, for the pious and the devout among us. A tavern sits on the edge of town, where people can spend the night or the evening. We also have a few houses with families living in them. Beyond these, the caravan slowly begins to settle in.

The caravan is a sight to see. There must be dozens of traders. Some of them are riding horses, others are riding donkeys. There are even a few carts and carriages, not to mention all the people who are on foot. The scent of foreign spices lingers on the breeze, and the air is full of strange languages I've never heard before. There are brilliant colors everywhere and so many interesting-looking people.

The caravan is made of a motley group that travels the world, city to city, even passing through small villages like mine. Some of the people settle down in the villages they pass through, while others join to travel so that there is no end to the strange and exotic things they carry.

A pair of guards passes by me and I long to know what stories they could tell me. There are many soldiers with the caravan. Their role is extremely important. The caravan is the driving force behind our economy, and the soldiers protect it from creatures and thieves alike. Without their protection, our way of life would be in great danger.

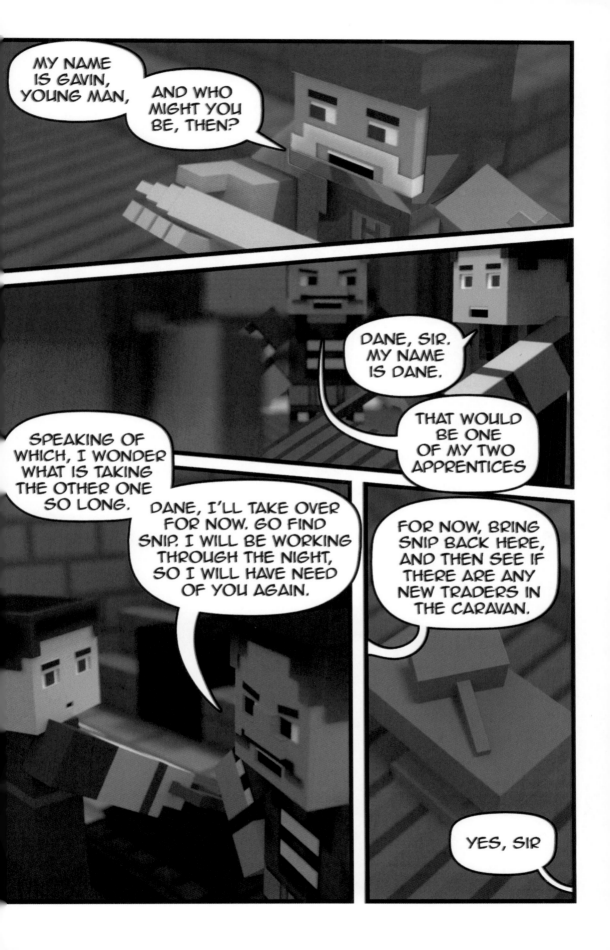

PEOPLE ARE EITHER JUST starting to unpack their belongings or have already created their makeshift market stalls, spreading their wares across colorful blankets. Small fires are scattered throughout the encampment, with weary travelers gathered around, setting up their camps for the night.

I spot Snip trading with one of the armor merchants. I hurry toward him. Snip finishes exchanging a chestplate for a bag of emeralds and turns to see me approach.

"Dane, what's the matter?"

"Viegar is wondering what is taking you so long," I say, crossing my arms over my chest. "You should get back to the smithee."

Snip rolls his eyes and shifts his weight onto one foot. "Dane, for someone who is always slacking off, you sure know how to order others around, don't you think? Anyway, I just sold the last of our chestplates, so we can head back now."

As Snip starts off, one of the merchants calls to me, "Hey you, boy. You look like a strong lad. Care to help me with this?" The voice hails from an old man who is leaning heavily on a walking stick and looks about to fall over at any moment. "I've been walking for hours, and my back isn't what it used to be. Would you mind giving me a hand setting up camp?"

I look back toward Snip and he shrugs and holds up his bag of gold. "I have to get back. I'll see you at the shop."

I help the old man take the chests off his donkey, and then, while he unpacks, I start a fire. I smile to myself. It seems I've found a practical use for my blacksmith training. The old man offers me a pork chop and some bread. "Would you like some?" he asks, smiling.

My stomach growls. "Are you sure?"

"Of course, young lad, don't you worry about me. I have more than enough food with me to make sure I will not go to sleep hungry—enough to feed a few others too! This is not my first trip with the caravan, you know. I have learned to come prepared." He hands me the food on a cloth napkin.

I take a bite of pork. It's cool, salty, and satisfying. "How long have you been traveling with the caravan?" I ask.

"Well . . . everything put together, I think this is my . . ." He counts the memories in his head. ". . .Twenty-ninth trip in about forty years." He carefully lays the slice of pork over his bread and eats it like a sandwich.

My eyes widen. I forget my table etiquette and speak with my mouth full, "If you've been in the caravan so long, you must have a lot of good stories then, don't you?"

The old man smiles, a fond twinkle in his eye, and I flush at my manners. I swallow quickly, trying to hide my embarrassment. "Oh, I have a few stories," he says. "Would you like to hear some?"

I nod fiercely and take a big bite into my pork as my new companion clears his voice and begins to share his stories. He tells me his name is Kent, and he offers me one story after the other. I listen excitedly, my smile growing in amazement with every adventure: great stories about powerful creatures watching from the shadows, and incredible people shaping our world.

His words resonate within me, filling me with the kind of excitement and joy that blacksmithing never could. This is the life I want to live. Traveling on trade routes, exploring the lands, meeting new people and helping them . . . but as the moon shines high in the sky, I realize that there are responsibilities that I am expected to fulfill. I thank the man for his stories and the food, and he thanks me for the company. "It's nice to meet someone who'll listen to an old man's stories. Thank you."

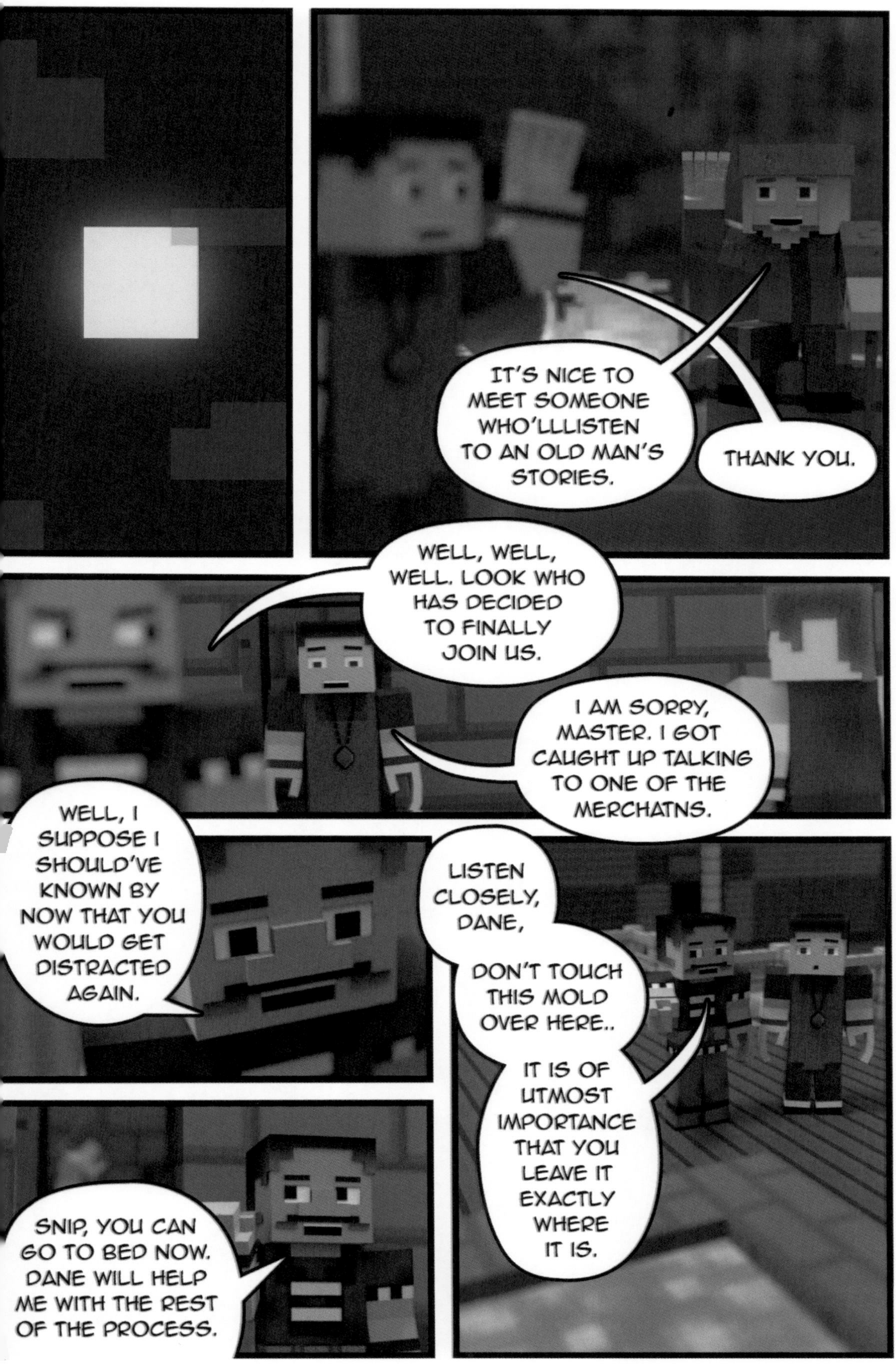
IT'S NICE TO MEET SOMEONE WHO'LLLISTEN TO AN OLD MAN'S STORIES.
THANK YOU.
WELL, WELL, WELL. LOOK WHO HAS DECIDED TO FINALLY JOIN US.
I AM SORRY, MASTER. I GOT CAUGHT UP TALKING TO ONE OF THE MERCHATNS.
WELL, I SUPPOSE I SHOULD'VE KNOWN BY NOW THAT YOU WOULD GET DISTRACTED AGAIN.
LISTEN CLOSELY, DANE,
DON'T TOUCH THIS MOLD OVER HERE..
IT IS OF UTMOST IMPORTANCE THAT YOU LEAVE IT EXACTLY WHERE IT IS.
SNIP, YOU CAN GO TO BED NOW. DANE WILL HELP ME WITH THE REST OF THE PROCESS.

AS I ENTER THE shop, Viegar is already working the forge, his back to the entrance. Snip crouches at the bellows—the mark of a truly exhausted apprentice. He sleepily works the handles up and down and with a jolt of guilt, I remember that Viegar is completing an overnight order for that knight.

Viegar barely glances over his shoulder as the door closes behind me. "Well, well, well. Look who has decided to finally join us."

I look down at the floor, my cheeks growing hot with shame. "I am sorry, master. I got caught up talking to one of the merchants."

Viegar sighs. "Well, I suppose I should've known by now that you would get distracted *again*. Snip, you can go to bed now. Dane will help me with the rest of the process."

Snip nods, yawning, and heads for the stairs to our rooms.

The master blacksmith is silent as he finishes examining what he has been working on. I apologize again, but Viegar ignores me. He sets the item down and removes his leather smock and protective gloves, taking care to set them on the worktable away from the forge's heat.

"Listen closely, Dane," he says. "Don't touch this mold, it is of utmost importance that you leave it where it is."

I approach slowly, to see what he's gesturing to. The heat is intense, I have to blink soot from my eyes. Over the lava pit, Viegar placed a stone mold, where a blazing molten metal glows.

It is amazing how raw materials, when heated to the right temperatures, become liquid and malleable. How a few relatively simple tools and the right motion of a hammer can turn worthless stone into a razor-edged axe, sharp enough to cut trees. How raw iron ore can be made into a chestplate strong enough to stop an arrow mid-flight. How a million grains of sand can be melted and turned into a glass bottle that can hold all kinds of liquid, even magic potions.

I look up and see Viegar watching me to make sure I've heard his instructions. I nod quickly, determined not to fail again.

"It needs to cool down later, but for now it has to stay at exactly this temperature," Viegar says, "I have an errand to run. Keep the forge running, I'll be back within a few hours. You don't have to do anything else, just make sure the forge does not die down."

Viegar puts on his cloak and ventures into the night. Curious as I am about where he is going, I can't leave this time around.

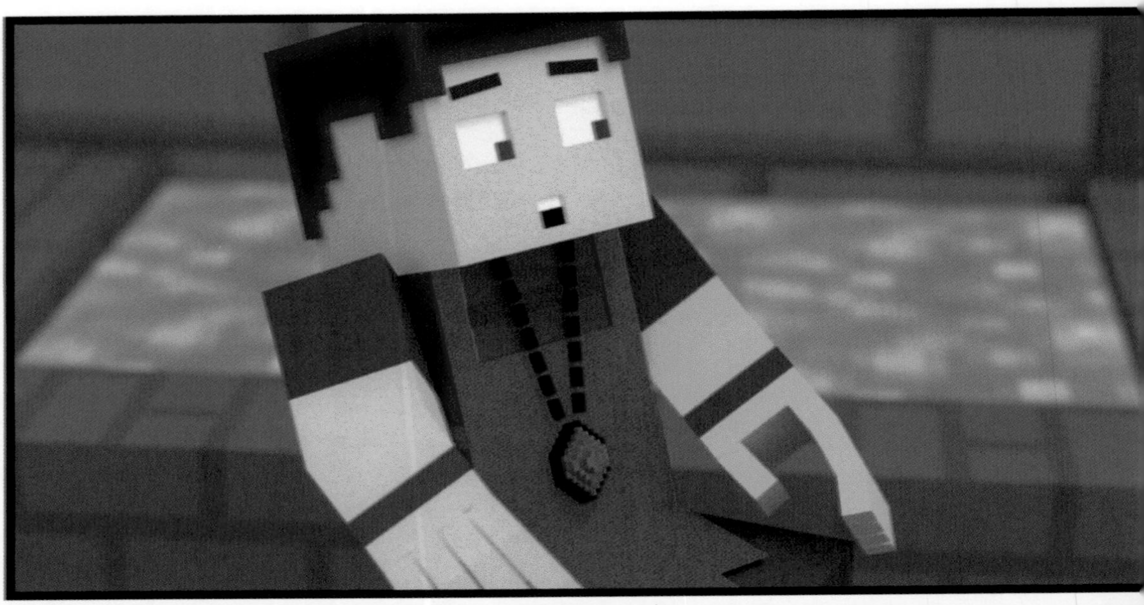

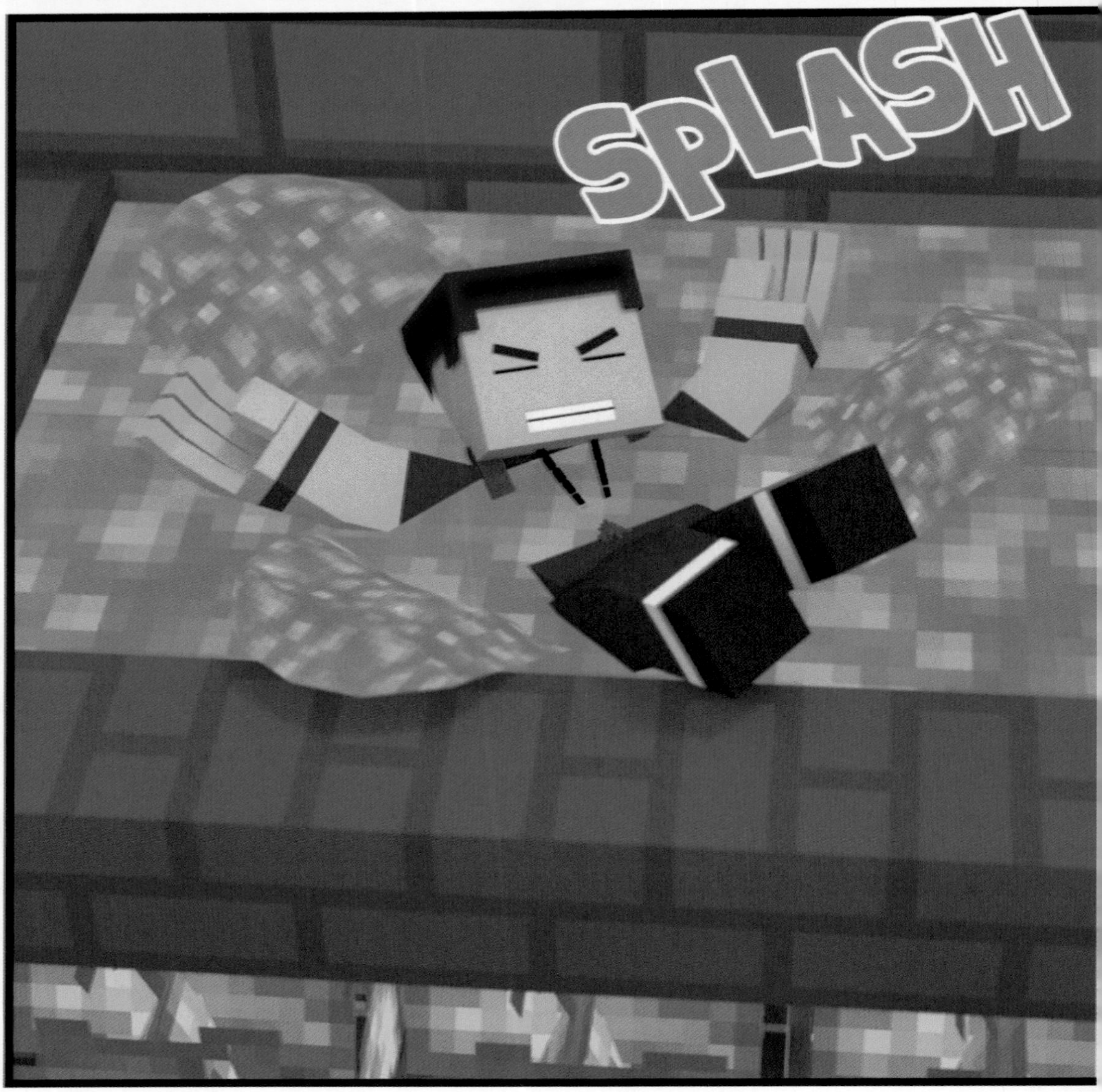
SPLASH

LEFT ON MY OWN, it's quiet in the forge. The flames crackle a steady, soft rhythm and throw flickering orange light across the walls. I sit in a chair near Viegar's project. It must be the order the knight commissioned. Only the most experienced are given the opportunity to join the Royal Guard. I wonder what adventures he's been through, how he earned his place among the Royal Guard, and what he will do with this new item once it is finished. In my mind, I go on these journeys with him, battling horrific creatures and traveling to the farthest corners of the cube. Before I realize it, my wandering mind leaves my head in a slumber. The molten metal in the forge slowly starts to cool.

"Dane! Why are you sleeping?!"

I jump up and my chair falls backward.

Viegar runs from the door, throwing off his cloak and pulling on his gloves. "Quickly, Dane, get more charcoal, we need to make sure the embers don't die down!"

I run for the charcoal pile on the other side of the shop. But my mind is still foggy with sleep and alarm. In my haste, I step on a stray lump of charcoal. My foot jerks painfully to the side, and I hit the forge as I fall. The molten metal in the mold bubbles violently. Sparks fly and a loud bang nearly deafens me. An immense burning sensation bursts across my skin;

agony sears through me. I feel as though I've been dropped straight into the heat of the forge. I want to shout, but I can't make a sound. I slip into darkness.

The next thing I know, I'm jolting awake in an unfamiliar bed. I gasp for air and inhale deeply. The dark spots in my vision begin to fade, and I realize I am in Viegar's bed and Viegar, Snip, and the knight, Gavin, sit at my bedside.

Viegar lets out a sigh of relief and turns to the knight, "I am so glad you were right, Gavin. He woke up after all."

I sit up straight. "What happened?"

There is a long pause as they all seem to silently debate who should answer. Finally Gavin speaks. "To be honest, we're not sure."

"You almost fell into the furnace!" Viegar says, "The molten metal spilled over you. You should be dead!" He glares at me, and I am unsure if it's because I made such a huge mistake or he'd rather I had been killed. "You had us all worried," he adds, to clear up my confusion.

"But . . . I'm still alive? How?" I look at my hands. They tingle, but the burning sensation is mostly gone, now. However, that is the least of my concerns; my hands are covered in a shining layer of silver. "What the—" I stretch out my arms before me;

the silver goes up under my sleeves. I haul up the edge of my tunic—my stomach is covered! I throw off my blanket and see my toes, gleaming like polished spoons. My entire body is covered in the stuff! The contents of that case of molten metal last night are now covering my entire body! It was hot enough to melt clean through armor and somehow I got it all over myself. "I'm still alive?!"

Gavin reaches into one of his pockets. "This might have something to do with it. I kept it safe for you." Out of his pocket, he pulls my mother's necklace. "I'm wondering where you got it. It's beautifully crafted."

"It was my mother's. She disappeared when I was little and left it for me. It's enchanted to lessen pain and heal damage faster."

Gavin hands me the necklace. "If it is an heirloom from your mother, then I am glad it was somehow untouched," he says. He stares at me as if he can hardly believe his eyes. "Your entire body was covered in glowing, molten metal. The glow has subsided, but the metal remains."

Gavin turns to Viegar. "The council will want to hear of this."

Viegar nods.

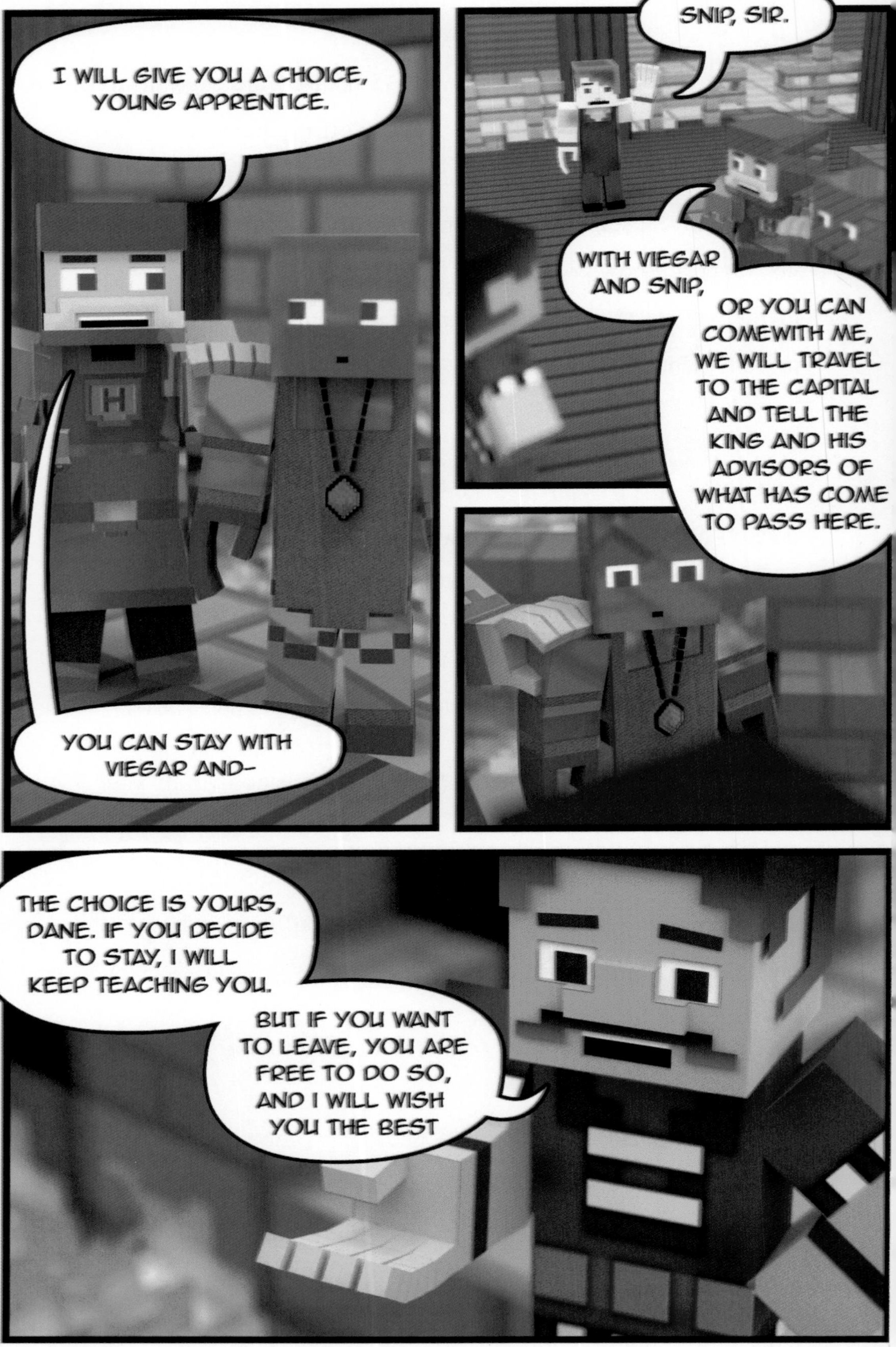
I WILL GIVE YOU A CHOICE, YOUNG APPRENTICE.
YOU CAN STAY WITH VIEGAR AND-
SNIP, SIR.
WITH VIEGAR AND SNIP,
OR YOU CAN COMEWITH ME, WE WILL TRAVEL TO THE CAPITAL AND TELL THE KING AND HIS ADVISORS OF WHAT HAS COME TO PASS HERE.
THE CHOICE IS YOURS, DANE. IF YOU DECIDE TO STAY, I WILL KEEP TEACHING YOU.
BUT IF YOU WANT TO LEAVE, YOU ARE FREE TO DO SO, AND I WILL WISH YOU THE BEST
H

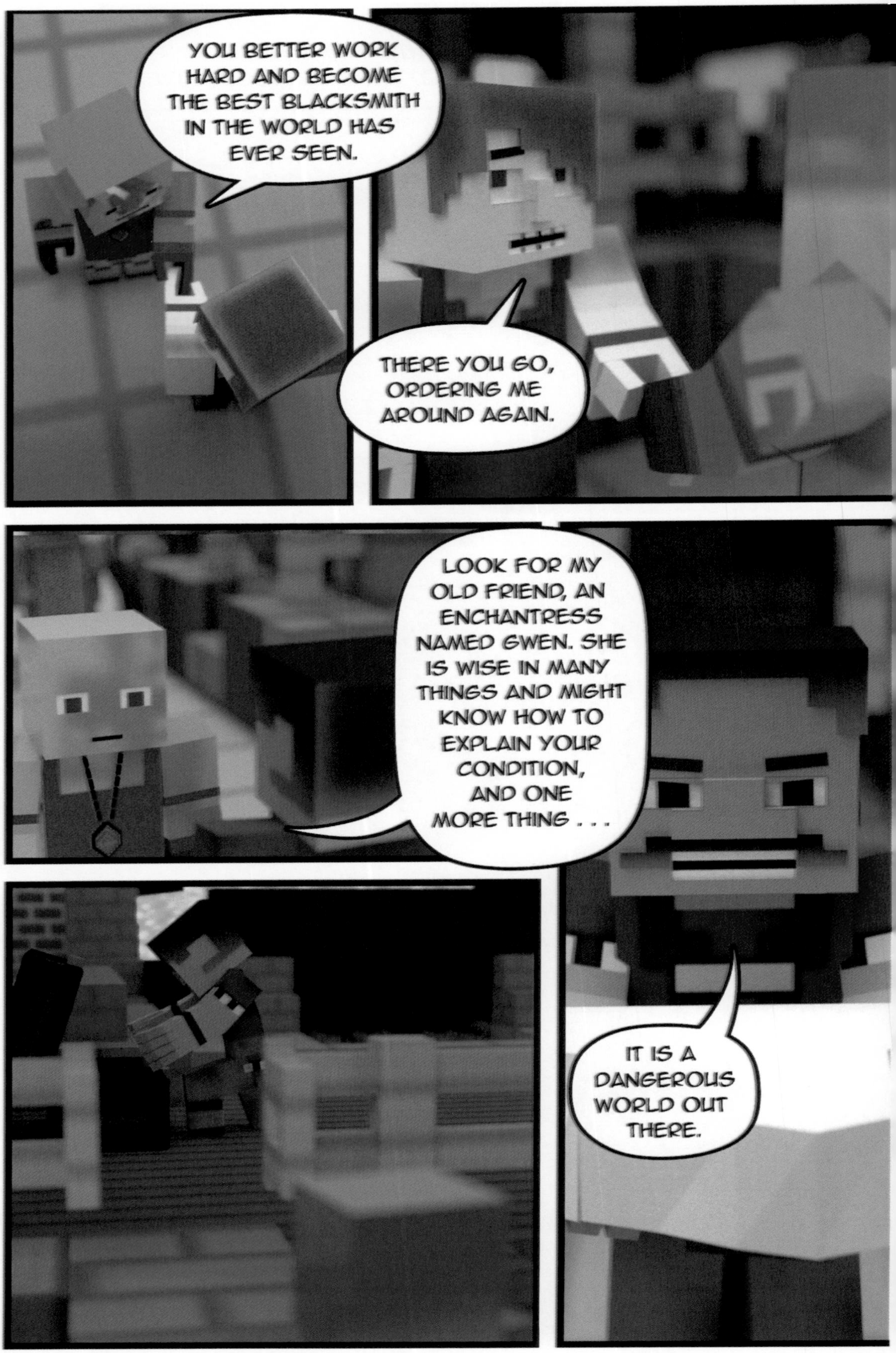
YOU BETTER WORK HARD AND BECOME THE BEST BLACKSMITH IN THE WORLD HAS EVER SEEN.
THERE YOU GO, ORDERING ME AROUND AGAIN.
LOOK FOR MY OLD FRIEND, AN ENCHANTRESS NAMED GWEN. SHE IS WISE IN MANY THINGS AND MIGHT KNOW HOW TO EXPLAIN YOUR CONDITION, AND ONE MORE THING . . .
IT IS A DANGEROUS WORLD OUT THERE.

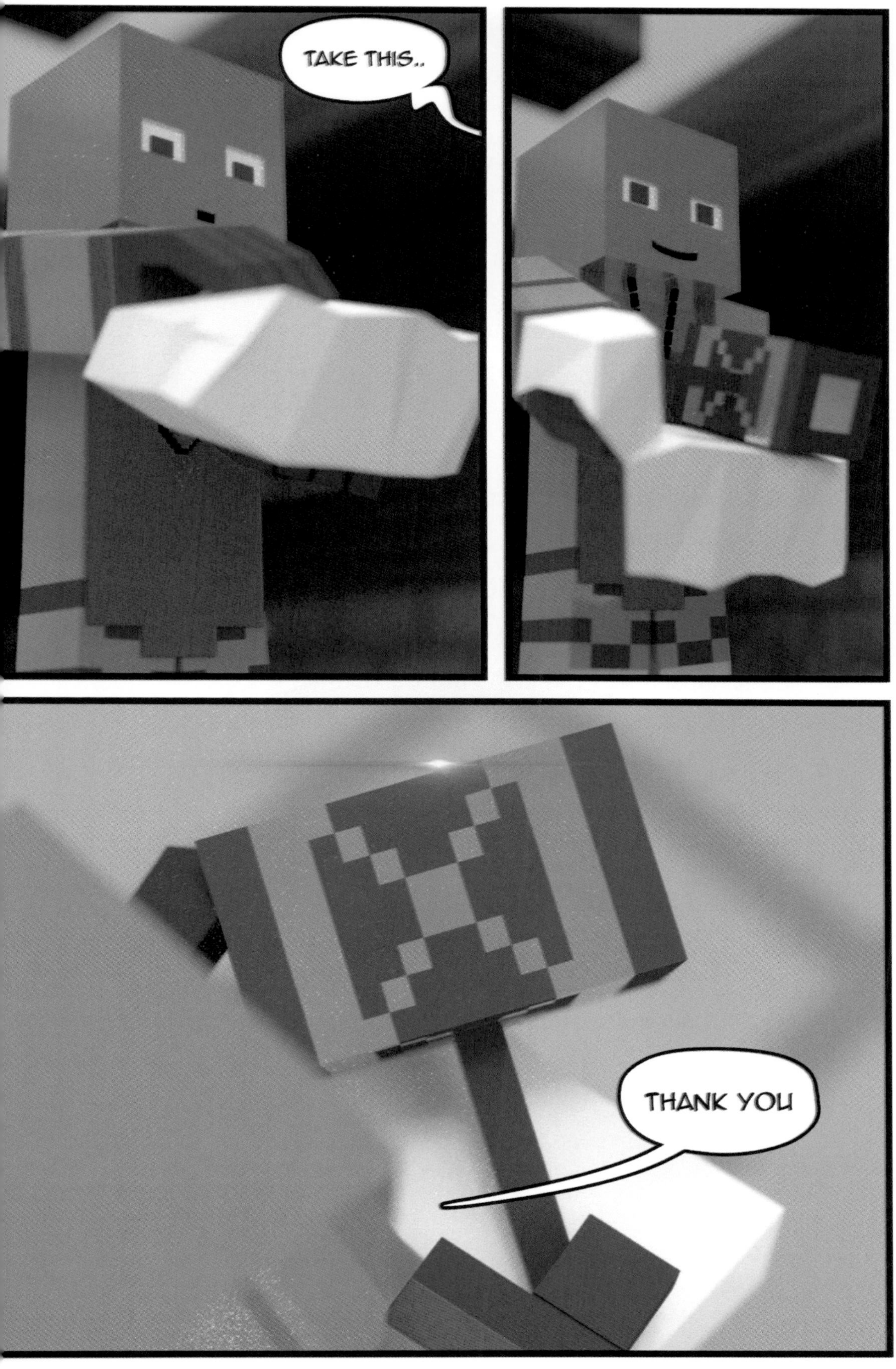
TAKE THIS..
THANK YOU

"WE CANNOT FORGE IT. It's too unstable. We have to find another solution. Before giving the Quicksilver to you, we tried to forge small weapons and arrowtips with it, but to no avail . . ." Gavin trails off.

The blacksmith looks at the knight and narrows his eyes. "I've seen that look before, Gavin. Something is bothering you, isn't it?"

The knight smiles and chuckles sardonically. "You know me too well, old friend." His smile turns to a frown and he sighs. "It's a long shot. But it's the only way to explain this. Magic must be involved somehow, and this is not your ordinary enchantment. If you'll allow it, I'd like to bring Dane with me. Just in case. The council has more knowledge on this matter than you and I do."

Viegar frowns. "Very well, I will allow it. If Dane wishes to accompany you, he is free to go."

Gavin then turns to me and claps a hand on my shoulder. "I will give you a choice, young apprentice. You can stay with Viegar and—" He looks in Snip's direction.

"Snip, sir," Snip says, flushing under his freckles.

"With Viegar and Snip," Gavin corrects as he looks back to me. "Or you can come with me. We will travel to the capital and tell the king and his advisors of what has come to pass here."

More than anything I want to say yes. I look at Viegar, torn between dreams and responsibility.

He shrugs, "The choice is yours, Dane. If you decide to stay, I will keep teaching you. But if you want to leave, you are free to do so, and I will wish you the best."

There isn't much choice to be made, traveling with a knight from the Royal Guard is a dream come true! Besides, I'm curious about my mother's necklace. I would've never dreamed my treasured heirloom could lead me into an adventure, but I am determined to discover all I can. "It would be an honor to go with you, sir," I say to the knight.

"Very well, then," Gavin says with a smile. "Go pack a bag. We leave with the caravan in an hour."

Without thinking, I jump out of bed, only to promptly stumble back. I feel so surprisingly well, that I'd almost forgotten how I've changed. My whole body feels heavier than before. I steady myself on my feet before I grab my small backpack, and start to pack the things I think I'll need. I pack flint and steel, a coil of rope, and a few apples.

It's a little strange, moving when my weight has changed so suddenly. Every time I reach for something I see the gleam of my hands and the strangeness of what's happened to me hits me again. My thoughts run wild, flitting between excitement and nervousness.

This place has been my home, yet here I am, rushing to leave it all behind. Viegar hasn't always been nice to me, but he has shown me that he cares by teaching me his craft. Not many people would make the effort he has. And fewer would throw away an opportunity to learn from a true master.

Am I supposed to be feeling some sort of regret? I think so. I'm sure my decision would disappoint my father, but he was once a Royal Guard. He might have meant the best for me when he left me to apprentice in the blacksmith trade, but he can hardly speak ill of me for following in his stead! And besides, by going with Gavin I might be able to help the Royal Guard. I slip my mother's necklace around my neck and touch the pendant, rubbing the stone between my fingers, while my thumb runs over her name. I am following in her stead too.

Snip, Viegar, and Gavin stand at the open door to the forge. I reach out a silvery hand to Snip. "You better work hard and become the best blacksmith the world has ever seen," I say.

Snips rolls his eyes and takes my hand, shaking it. "There you go, ordering me around again." But he's smiling fondly.

Viegar approaches me before I get any nearer to Gavin. He speaks quietly, "Look for my old friend, an enchantress named Gwen. She is wise in many things and might know how to explain your condition. And one more thing . . ." He holds up a finger and quickly hurries to one of his chests. He returns with something wrapped in a small blanket. He pulls away the cloth to reveal a broad hammer. "It is a dangerous world out there. Take this."

I glance at him and at the gift. I know it was forged with the utmost care, as is everything Viegar makes. I can think of no way to express my gratitude for such an amazing gift. "Thank you," I stammer, as I accept the hammer.

I carry the hammer reverently. Gavin holds the door open for me and I walk through. The door closes behind me, and I see my village spread out before me. Tears well in my eyes. Boring as this life might be, it is all I have ever known. I wipe away the tears before Gavin can see.

The knight leads the way through the village and I follow, silently saying my goodbyes to all the people and places I've known.

We reach the edge of the caravan encampment. Most people are already up, packed and ready to go. The knight helps me onto his horse, a spotted brown steed with a diamond caparison.

The horse seems uneasy about my weight. "Easy, girl," Gavin says as he strokes her mane a bit. "Dane is a friend." I make myself comfortable and hold my mother's necklace close to my heart. Shouts go down the line of carts and one by one they rock into motion.

My heart hammers in my chest, and all fear and doubt flee from my mind. It's happening, my adventure is about to start! I glance down at Gavin and find him quietly patting the horse's neck. He too is looking into the distance, a thoughtful frown on his face. He catches me watching him and offers up a smile that doesn't quite meet his eyes. "Are you ready for a journey?" He asks.

I nod eagerly, too excited to let his unexplained melancholy get to me. I look ahead as our horse starts into a trot, following the caravan.

This is the first day of my new life as an adventurer.

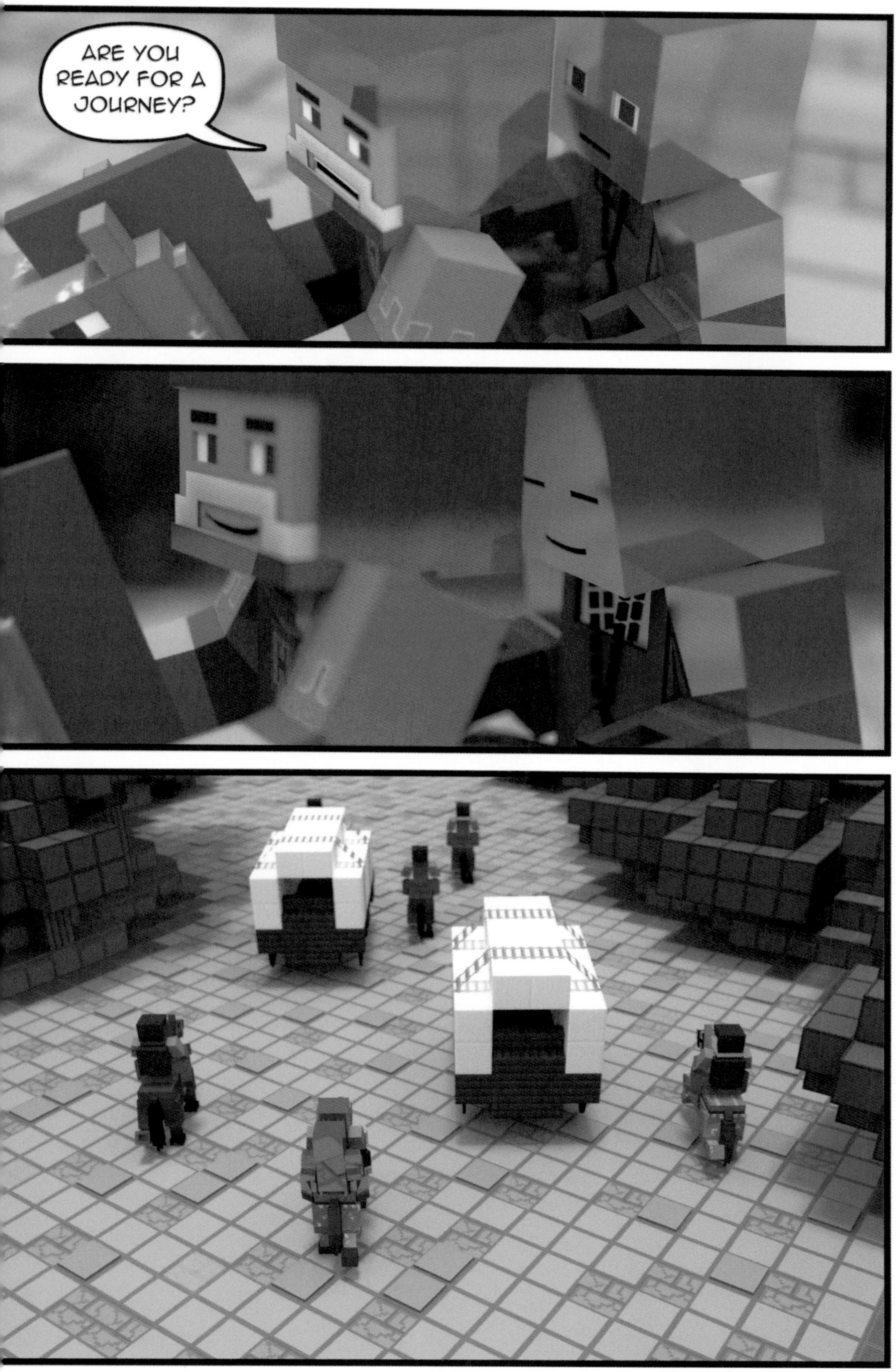
ARE YOU READY FOR A JOURNEY?

NEXT!

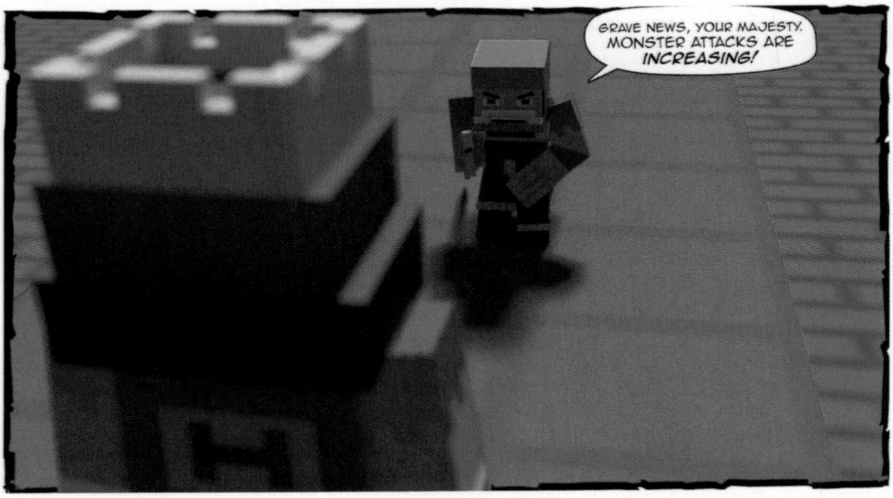
GRAVE NEWS, YOUR MAJESTY. MONSTER ATTACKS ARE *INCREASING!*

Legends and Heroes Issue 3: Kingdom at War! Get it here StoneMarshall.com/l&h0003

Rate and review. If you enjoyed this story and want more, give us a 5-star rating. Thanks!

Solve the puzzle. Uncover secrets!

StoneMarshall.com/lh0001-puzzle

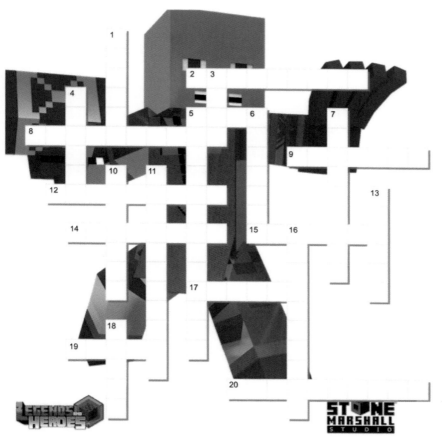

Across
2. Dane wishes he could go on an ...
5. The better blacksmith's apprentice.
8. Armor worn on the upper part of a body.
9. The material Viegar crafts; he says Dane's not ready for it yet.
12. Another name for monsters roaming south of the Kingdom.
14. Material Viegar asked Dane to use to keep the forge burning.

15. Monsters hide here.
17. The tool Viegar gives to Dane as he leaves with Gavin.
19. A furnace used by a blacksmith to heat metals.
20. The job for which Snip is training.

Down

1. Gavin is a royal...
3. Young apprentice to Viegar who wishes he could go on adventures!
4. The master blacksmith.
5. The creator of Legends and Heroes.
6. Who left Viegar in charge of Dane? Dane's ...
7. The village where Viegar, Snip, and Dane live.
10. Group of villagers who travel the Kingdom trading and bartering resources.
11. The material discovered by the alchemist, Stella, that coats Dane, making his skin stronger than diamond armor.
13. Viegar is a ... blacksmith.
16. Dane's job under his master blacksmith.
18. The Stone of Ultimate Power!
(Hint: This is the stone Gwen tells Meta about in Issue 2)

Word Key
ADVENTURE **APPRENTICE** BLACKSMITH **BREGU**
CARAVAN **CHARCOAL** CHESTPLATE **CREATURES**
DANE **DIAMOND** FORGE **HAMMER** KNIGHT **MASTER**
PARENTS **QUICKSILVER** SHADOWS **SNIP**
STATHMORE **STONEMARSHALL** VIEGAR

ABOUT STONE MARSHALL

You've read the story, now enter the world. Get maps, character information, updates and bonuses! Subscribe to get Stone Marshall Club News:

StoneMarshall.com/club

Everything I do:

StoneMarshall.com

StoneMarshallStudio.com

The Stone Marshall Studio, an awesome team making awesome stuff.

Flynn's Log

STONE MARSHALL
Flynn's Log

In the near future, video games begin to change and evolve. Virtual intelligence takes over the digital world and creates a digital crisis, bringing the real world to a halt. The only person who can save the world is Flynn, but he needs help from his friends, the Hackers.

StoneMarshall.com/Flynns_Log

Created and written by

STONE MARSHALL®

Legends & Heroes

LEGENDS AND HEROES

Ever wonder what life is like in Minecraft?

In the cube, a secret war is waged as Legends battle Heroes for control. Legends seek to darken the cube while Heroes fight to defend it. If Legends win, the game will never be safe for players again.

StoneMarshall.com/L&H

Created by Stone Marshall, with the Stone Marshall Studio

STONE MARSHALL® STUDIO

Printed in Great Britain
by Amazon

23983194R00030